This igloo book belongs to:

....

Contents

Published in 2011
by Igloo Books Ltd
Cottage Farm
Sywell
Northants
NN6 0BJ
www.igloo-books.com

F021 1111
10 9 8 7 6 5 4 3
ISBN: 978-0-85734-497-7

Printed and manufactured in China
Illustrated by Garyfalia Leftheri
Stories by Melanie Joyce

Stories for 5 Year Olds

igloo

The Best Den, Ever

Meg lived with her mummy, near a big wood. "Can I build a den in the wood, today?" asked Meg. But, Mummy shook her head and said, "You can't go into the woods by yourself, Meg. I'm a bit busy to help you make a den today. Maybe we'll do it tomorrow."

Meg felt a bit disappointed, so she went next door to see if her best friend, Mimi, wanted to play.

Meg and Mimi played catch and it was fun. But then, the ball rolled right up to the edge of the wood. "It looks so lovely and pretty in there," said Meg. "I'm not by myself, so I'm sure Mummy wouldn't mind if we have a little look." So, she stepped into the trees with Mimi following behind.

All around, birds twittered and leaves rustled. "Let's build a den," said Meg and she ran off to a big, old tree to pick up sticks. But, up in the tree something was moving. Suddenly, there was a very loud rapping and a tapping, then a drilling and a hammering. "What's that?" asked Meg, covering her ears.

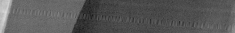

"It's a monster!" cried Mimi, pointing up at a shadow on the big, tree trunk. "Now it's moving!"

Meg jumped up and looked at the shadow. "Quick, run!" she cried. So, the two friends scampered off, as fast as they could, over the leaves, between the trees, further into the shady wood.

7

When they stopped, Meg looked round and asked, "Where are we?"
"I don't know," replied Mimi, "but I want to go home now, I'm scared."

Meg was a bit scared, too. But then, she heard someone calling.
"Meg, Mimi, where are you?" It was Mum. She had come to look for
Meg and Mimi.

"I told you not to go off into the woods," said Mum, hugging them tight. Meg told Mum all about the den and the monster in the tree. Mum just smiled and said, "It's only the woodpecker. He's not scary at all."

Then, Mum held their hands. "Come on, you two," she said. "Let's go home and we'll all make a den together."

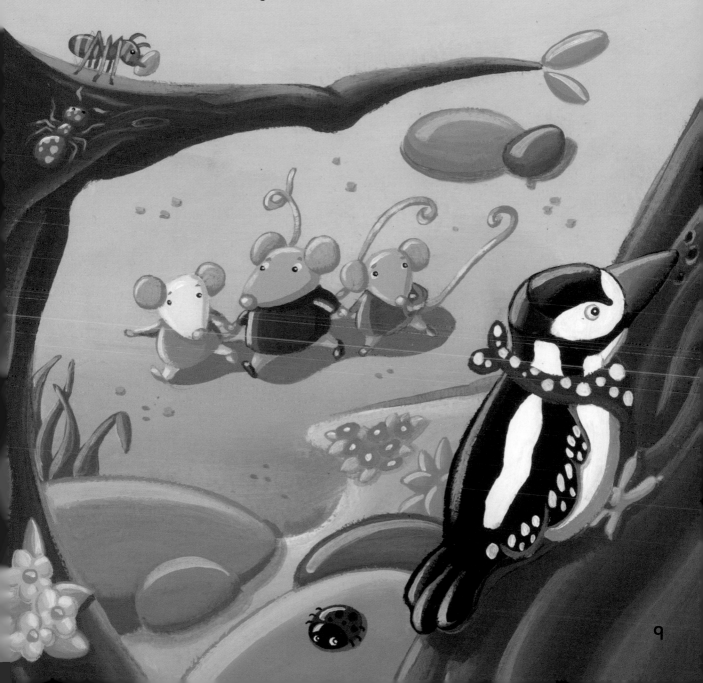

At home, Mum got out all the useful, den-making things. There were frayed, old sheets and soft, woolly blankets. She even had cushions and an old china tea-set. Before long, Meg and Mimi were sitting, cosily, in their brand new den.

Mum brought them juice and a dish of cookies. "I'm glad that you are safely back home," she said. "I want you to promise me that you'll never go into the woods without a grown-up again."

"We promise," said Meg and Mimi. It had been very exciting in the woods, but, at home, they had the best den ever.

Tania's Tutu

Tania wanted to look like a proper ballerina, so she rummaged in her dressing-up box. But, Mum's old skirt was raggy and torn. The too-big ballet shoes were scuffed and worn. "I don't look like a proper ballerina at all," said Tania. Then, two fat tears rolled down her cheeks.

"What's the matter?" asked Mum.
"I'm not a proper ballerina," wailed Tania, as she sniffled and snuffled.
So, Mum just gave her a great big cuddle. "Don't worry," she said, smiling.
"Come with me. I'll help you to look like a proper ballerina."

13

Mum took Tania to see her friend, Lizzy. Tania and Lizzy played in the sandpit and built sandcastles, while their mums had a chat in the kitchen.

When it was time to leave, Tania noticed that Mum was holding a neatly wrapped parcel. "What is it?" she asked. But, Mum just said, "It's a surprise."

14

Next, Mum took Tania to Billy's house. Tania and Billy played for ages on the swings and slide. Tania was having such fun, she forgot all about her tutu. Then, Mum came out with a mysterious box. "What's that?" asked Tania. "It's a surprise," said Mum. "Come on, it's time to go."

At home, Mum opened the box. "Billy's mum had this in the attic," she said. The box was full of slinky silk cloth, buttons, beads and shiny pink ribbon. "We'll use all of this to make you a very special tutu," said Mum.

So, Mum stitched and sewed and Tania stuck on sequins.

At last, Tania's tutu was finished. It was pink and frilly and very sparkly. Tania looked in the mirror. "It's lovely, thank you, Mummy," she said.

Then, Mum unwrapped the strangely shaped parcel. "These ballet shoes are too small for Lizzy," she said, "so she's given them to you." Tania was very happy. "I want to dance and dance," she said.

Just then, the doorbell rang. It was Lizzy, Billy and their mums. "Surprise!" they said. Lizzy had put on her tutu and Billy had brought some music. "Now that you've got your new tutu, we can put on a show," they said.

18

That afternoon, Tania danced in her lovely, new tutu. She pointed her toes, held up her arms and waved her hands. Then, she whirled and twirled until she finished with a very graceful bow. Everyone clapped and cheered. "Well done, Tania," they said. "Now you really are a proper ballerina!"

Tent Pegs

Danny and Sam wanted to have adventures and stay out all night, just like the superheroes in their comic books. So, they went downstairs to ask Mum and Dad if they could. "Alright," said Mum and Dad, smiling at one another, "we'll put a tent up for you in the garden."

Dad searched in a cupboard and pulled out an old tent and a bag full of poles and pegs. "Here we are," he said. "This is a proper adventurer's tent," and he went into the garden to put it up.

Then, Mum gave Danny and Sam some sandwiches and a big bottle of orange juice. "These are just in case you get hungry," she said.

Outside, in the garden, Danny and Sam settled inside the old tent. "This is exciting," they said. Then, they both sat and waited. Soon, the sun began to sink and shadows stretched, like long fingers, across the grass. Then, the sky grew dark and the night crept in.

22

"Brrr… " said Sam, shivering. "It's a bit chilly. Let's have some sandwiches and a drink." So, they tucked into their sandwiches and drank their juice. Danny and Sam were just enjoying them when there was a rustling and a hooting noise outside. Then, something large flew past the tent.

"What was that?" asked Sam and he clicked on his torch. But there was nothing outside. So, they snuggled down into their soft, sleeping bags.

All was quiet for a while. Then, Danny saw something crawling up the tent. But, there wasn't just one thing — there were loads.

"Urgh! Crawly monsters!" he said, jumping up and shaking his torch.
"I don't like being a superhero," said Danny. "It's too cold and I'm scared."
Suddenly, the tent flap flicked back. "I've just come to see if you are alright,"
said Dad.

"No! We aren't," said Danny and Sam. They told Dad all about the hooty noise and the creepy monsters.

"The hooting was just the owl," said Dad. "The monsters are only garden snails. If you are worried, I can stay out here and keep you company."

26

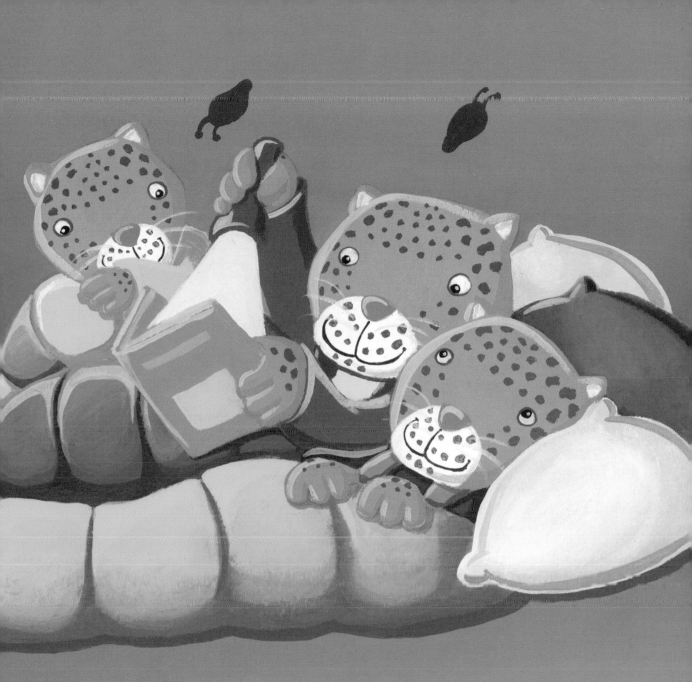

"Yes, please," said Danny and Sam. So, Dad got his sleeping bag and they all snuggled down. Then Dad told them stories by torchlight. Before long, everyone was cozy and warm. "Thank you, Dad," said Danny. "Thank you," said Sam. Now they felt like proper adventurers.

Noah's Adventure

Noah the dolphin was playing hide-and-seek amongst the coral with his best friend, Sophie the shark.

"5..4..3..2..1.. coming!" said Noah and he flicked his tail and went to look for his friend. Noah searched all over, amongst the swishy seaweed and the bright coral, but he couldn't find Sophie anywhere.

Suddenly, there was a noise from behind a rock. "Found you, Sophie!" cried Noah, poking his head round. But, it wasn't Sophie, it was a beady-eyed crab who snapped, angrily, with his giant claws. "Oh, no!" said Noah and he dashed off into the seaweed.

Just then, a swirling shoal of silvery fish dashed past. "Hello," said Noah, "have you seen my friend, Sophie?" But the shoal shot off.
"Quick, swim away, he's coming!" they cried.

"Who's coming?" asked Noah. Then, he saw the great shadow of the big, blue whale swimming towards him, with his mouth open wide.

30

"Oh, dear," said Noah and his swishy tail shivered and his little fins quivered. Then, with a flick, he darted off after the silvery shoal. "Wait for me!" he cried, as he saw the fish disappear into a big, dark shipwreck that sat on the bottom of the sea.

But, inside the wreck, there was no sign of the fish. Everything was quiet. Then, there was a strange, glooping sound. "Hello," said Noah, "is there anybody here?" But no one answered.

The shipwreck was full of strange shapes and wobbly shadows. Suddenly, some of them began to move.

A cross-looking octopus came out of the shadows, waving its legs this way and that. "What are you doing here?" it asked. "This is my ship and it belongs to me. Go away." Then, the unfriendly octopus waved its long, wiggly legs to shoo poor Noah away.

Suddenly, deep in the shipwreck, something else moved.

"Excuse me," said a voice. "This shipwreck belongs to everybody." It was
Noah's friend, Sophie. She had been hiding in the shipwreck all the time.
When the octopus saw how big she was, he swam off without another word.

Noah was very happy to see his friend.

"Come on, Noah," said Sophie. "Let's go and play at home."
Noah was very relieved. He loved playing hide-and-seek, but he'd definitely
had enough excitement for one day!

Helpful Clive

One day, Mummy was too busy doing housework to play with Clive. "Maybe if I do things to help Mummy," said Clive, "she will have time to play with me." So, he went to the cupboard and got the vacuum cleaner. "I'll make the carpet look clean, just like Mummy does," he said, pushing a round button.

Suddenly, there was a *swoosh* and a *thwack* and all the flowers in Mum's brown vase disappeared up the long, silvery tube. Then, the vase rocked this way and that and toppled over, onto the carpet.
"I don't like the vacuum cleaner," said Clive and he pushed the button again and ran off outside.

It was sunny and hot in the garden. "Maybe I can help Mummy by watering the vegetables," said Clive. So, he went to the tap with the hosepipe attached and twisted and turned it, but nothing happened. So, Clive peered with one eye down the long, dark pipe.

There was a gurgle and a rush, then a gigantic *swoosh* and water burst out in a blast. The hosepipe wriggled and swayed like a long, blue snake. Poor Clive chased it this way and that. "I'm getting very wet," he said. "I think I'll turn off the tap."

Just then, Clive's best friend, Ned, appeared at the gate. "If you're not busy today," he said, "do you want to come and play?"
"Yes, please," replied Clive and he ran to the gate. But the grass was wet from the hosepipe water and Clive slipped and slid with a *splodge* right into the muddy, vegetable patch.

Ned gave a giggle. "Oh, Clive," he said. "You're very muddy. You'd better go and tell your mummy."

Just then, Clive heard a loud voice calling. "What have you been doing, Clive? My flowers have gone, the vase is broken and the carpet's all wet!"

Clive slunk into the kitchen, dripping. "I just wanted to help, so you'd have time to play with me," he said and he began to cry.

"Thank you, Clive," soothed Mum, in her softest voice. "You're a bit small to do housework all by yourself. Perhaps, next time, we'll do it together."

That afternoon, after Clive had put on some nice, dry clothes, Mum made some extra-special, delicious cookies. Ned came round and they all had lots of fun. Being helpful was all very well, but it wasn't nearly as exciting as playing hide-and-seek.

43

Charlie and the Cookies

Charlie loved cookies. He thought the best ones were the crunchy and buttery ones with delicious dollops of chocolate inside. Each night, after tea, Mum let Charlie have a cookie as a treat. Charlie always wanted another one, but Mum said, "No, Charlie, you shouldn't eat too many cookies."

One night, Charlie saw that Mum had forgotten to put the cookie jar back in the cupboard. "I'll just have a little taste," he said, reaching inside. He chewed and munched and soon a whole cookie was gone. So, Charlie took another and then another. Then, with his tummy all full, he crept upstairs to bed.

In the kitchen, Mum found the empty cookie jar. All along the kitchen floor was a trail of crunchy, buttery, chocolatey crumbs. "Hmm... " said Mum, "I wonder who's been dipping into the cookie jar? I think I can guess who," and she followed the trail of crumbs all the way upstairs.

In Charlie's room, there were some very strange sounds coming from under the quilt. "Ooh, ow, ouch," groaned a little voice.

"What's the matter, Charlie?" asked Mum.

"I've got stomach ache," replied Charlie, coming out from under the covers, "and it hurts."

"Well, Charlie," said Mum, softly, "now you know why it's not good to eat too many cookies."

47

Luckily, Mum had some special medicine to make Charlie's tummy-ache go away. Soon, he was settled down in bed, all comfy and warm. "Thank you, Mummy," said Charlie, as he drifted off to sleep.

Mum gently kissed him goodnight and she turned out the light. After that, Charlie never ate too many cookies again.